Kenya

Brazil

Kazakhstan

Turkey

Germany

For Debbi, the real Ms. Hirokane,
and for all the immigrants who helped build the U.S. and
continue to contribute in countless important ways. I raise my teacup to you. —A.W.

To my ESL class friends in Livonia, MI —H.Y.

Neal Porter Books

Text copyright © 2022 by Andrea Wang

Illustrations copyright © 2022 by Hyewon Yum

All Rights Reserved

HOLIDAY HOUSE is registered in the U.S. Patent and Trademark Office.

Printed and bound in December 2021 at Imago, Rawang, Malaysia.

The artwork for this book was created with colored pencils.

Book design by Jennifer Browne

www.holidayhouse.com

First Edition

1 3 5 7 9 10 8 6 4 2

Library of Congress Cataloging-in-Publication Data

Names: Wang, Andrea, author. | Yum, Hyewon, illustrator.

Title: Luli and the language of tea / written by Andrea Wang ; illustrated

by Hyewon Yum.

Description: First edition. | New York : Holiday House, [2022] | "A Neal

Porter book." | Audience: Ages 4 to 8. | Audience: Grades K–1.

Summary: While her parents attend a community ESL class, Luli connects

with other immigrant children by sharing a love of tea. Includes

author's note.

Identifiers: LCCN 2021004108 | ISBN 9780823446148 (hardcover)

Subjects: CYAC: Immigrants—Fiction. | Tea—Fiction. | Sharing—Fiction.

Classification: LCC PZ7.1.W3645 Lu 2022 | DDC [E]—dc23

LC record available at https://lccn.loc.gov/2021004108

ISBN: 978-0-8234-4614-8 (hardcover)

Luli

and the Language of Tea

Andrea Wang

Pictures by

Hyewon Yum

NEAL PORTER BOOKS

HOLIDAY HOUSE / NEW YORK

The playroom was quiet.
Luli couldn't speak English.
Neither could the others.

All around the room, children played alone.

Last time, Luli had played by herself, too,
until she had an idea.
She'd drawn it for Miss Hirokane.
This time, Luli had a plan.

From inside her backpack and
onto the round table Luli set

a thermos,

a canister,

stacks of cups,

and a fat-bellied teapot.

Out of the canister and
into the teapot
Luli dropped a small
ball of tea leaves.
Plop.

Out of the thermos and
over the tea leaves
Luli poured steaming
hot water.
Ploosh.

Luli took a deep breath.

"茶!" (*Chá!*) she
called in Chinese.

All around the room, heads popped up.

"Чай?" (*Chay?*) asked Maxim in Russian.

"चाय?" (*Ch-eye?*) Anaya said in Hindi.

"Çay?" (*Tch-eye?*) asked Kerem in Turkish.

"چای؟" (*Chah-ee?*) Nikou said in Persian.

"شيء؟" (*Shay?*) asked Hakim in Arabic.

"Té?" (*Tay?*) Valentina said in Spanish.

"Tee?" (*Tee?*) asked Matthias in German.

"Chai?" (*Ch-eye?*) Tishala said in Swahili.

"Chá?" (*Shah?*) asked Pedro in Portuguese.

The tea was ready.
Luli beamed.
She was ready.
"Chá!" She beckoned.

All around the room,
children joined together.

Luli poured the first cup and gave it to

Maxim, who gave it to

Hakim, who gave it to

Valentina, who gave it to

Matthias, who gave it to

Anaya, who gave it to

Kerem, who gave it to

Nikou, who gave it to

Tishala, who gave it to

Pedro.

All around the table,
children passed tea.

Everyone had a full cup.

Except Luli.

Pedro took Luli's empty cup
and passed it to

Tishala, who passed it to

Kerem, who passed it to

Nikou, who passed it to

Matthias, who passed it to

Hakim, who passed it to

Valentina, who passed it to

Maxim, who passed it to Luli.

Anaya, who passed it to

All around the table,
each child gave a little tea.

Now everyone had a share.
Hands curled around warm cups.
Mouths curved into shy smiles.

Luli took another deep breath and pulled out one last surprise. She held up a box and spoke her new favorite word. In English.

"Cookie?"

The playroom was no longer quiet.

Luli's teapot was empty,
but her heart was full.

A Note from the Author

I was born in the United States, but my parents were born in China. They came to the United States for the same reason most immigrants do—the chance of a better life. They learned English before they arrived, but they met many people who didn't. Both my parents helped those who couldn't speak English. My mother started a program that helped other immigrant nurses pass tests that allowed them to take care of patients. My father taught English as a Second Language (ESL) classes in high schools, nursing homes, and hospitals. I recorded myself reading the textbook aloud so my father's students could listen to my pronunciation.

Every visitor to my parents' home was offered tea and snacks. When I found out that the Chinese word for tea is similar to the word for tea in many other languages, I was intrigued. Why was this? How could asking for "chai" in India get you the same drink in Kenya, with some differences in flavor and spices? It turns out that the word for tea in over 200 languages can be traced back to two Chinese dialects. According to legend, tea was invented in China around 2700 BCE. (That's over 4,700 years ago.) As people around the world began to trade with China, they took tea and the word for it back to their homes. Over time, the pronunciation in different countries has changed, but not too much. And whether you say "cha," "tee," "tay," or "chai," you are drinking the same thing!

About the Children and Languages in This Story

All the children in this story are immigrants from countries where tea drinking is a large part of their culture. Although Ireland and the United Kingdom are among the world's biggest tea consumers, they are not included in this story because English is one of their official languages. The languages in this book have multiple dialects and regional variations. For example, Luli speaks a dialect of Chinese called Mandarin. I have tried to present the pronunciation of the most widely spoken dialect or official language of each particular country.

Asia: In 2019, there were more than 14 million Asian immigrants living in the U.S.

China: Luli (*LOO-lee*)

Some say that tea was discovered when leaves from the *Camellia sinensis* plant blew into Emperor Shen-Nung's pot of boiling water in 2737 BCE. The Chinese don't usually add anything to their tea.

Kazakhstan: Maxim (*Mak-SEEM*)

People here often drink hot black tea with milk or lemon and sugar from tea bowls instead of teacups.

India: Anaya (*Uh-NYE-ya*)

Like China, India is one of the world's largest producers of tea. People here like to add milk to black tea boiled with spices like cinnamon, cardamom, and ginger.

Turkey: Kerem (*KEH-rem*)

In 2016, Turks drank more tea per person than any other country in the world. They add sugar to their tea but never milk.

Iran: Nikou (*NEE-koo*)

In Iran, a traditional way of drinking the strong, bitter tea is to hold a sugar cube between your teeth and sip the tea through it, allowing the sugar to melt.

TURKEY

KAZAKHSTAN

IRAN

CHINA

INDIA

Africa: In 2019, there were more than 2.4 million African immigrants living in the U.S.

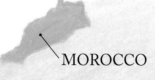

Morocco: Hakim (*Ha-KEEM*)

Moroccans like to drink green gunpowder tea mixed with fresh mint and sugar. Gunpowder tea doesn't actually have gunpowder in it—each tea leaf is rolled into a tiny round pellet. Together the pellets look like grains of gunpowder!

MOROCCO

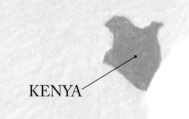

KENYA

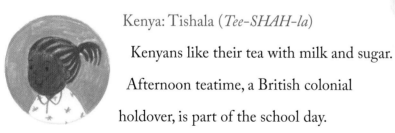

Kenya: Tishala (*Tee-SHAH-la*)

Kenyans like their tea with milk and sugar. Afternoon teatime, a British colonial holdover, is part of the school day.

Europe: In 2019, there were almost 4.7 million European immigrants living in the U.S.

GERMANY

Germany: Matthias (*Ma-TEE-as*)

In the East Frisia region of Germany, hot tea is poured over a lump of rock sugar in a teacup. Then, a spoonful of heavy cream is added, which bounces off the bottom and rises to the top to look like a cloud. You are not supposed to stir it all together before drinking it!

South America: In 2019, there were about 3.3 million South American immigrants living in the U.S.

BRAZIL

CHILE

Brazil: Pedro (*PAY-dro*)

Although Brazilians do drink tea, the most popular tea drink is called chá mate, which is made from the yerba mate plant instead of the Chinese tea plant.

Chile: Valentina (*Va-len-TEEN-ah*)

In Chile, teatime is called "onces," which means "elevenses," even though it occurs between 5:00 pm and 7:00 pm. In addition to tea, bread, cakes, pastries, cheese, or sandwiches may be served.

For a bibliography of works used, please visit andreaywang.com.

Morocco

Iran

China

Chile

India